by MARTY KELLEY

This book is for the Dynamic
Duo, Tahra and Avery – Marty

Published by Curious Fox, an imprint
of Capstone Global Library Limited,
264 Banbury Road, Oxford, OX2
7DY – Registered company number:
6695582

www.curious-fox.com

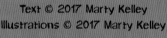

Text © 2017 Marty Kelley
Illustrations © 2017 Marty Kelley

The author's moral rights are
hereby asserted.

ISBN 978 1 782 02701 0
21 20 19 18 17
10 9 8 7 6 5 4 3 2 1

A CIP catalogue for this book is available from the
British Library.

Printed and bound in China.

Contents

All About Me!

A picture of me!

Name:
Molly Mac

People in my family:
Mum
Dad
Drooly baby brother Alex

My best friend: KAYLEY!!!!

I really like:
Crunchy delicious tacos!
But not if they have tomatoes on them.
Yuck! They are squirty and wet.

When I grow up I want to be:
An artist. And a famous animal trainer.
And a professional taco taster. And a teacher.
And a superhero. And a dinner lady. And a pirate!

My special memory: Kayley and I camped in my
garden. We toasted marshmallows with cheese.
They were surprisingly un-delicious.

Chapter 1

The Snack Bandit

Klunk!

Molly Mac climbed into her seat in Mr Rose's classroom.

Kayley sat down next to her. She looked up at Molly. Way, way up.

"Ummm... Molly?" asked Kayley.

"Don't ask," said Molly.

"I'm asking," said Kayley. "Why are you sitting on your lunch box? It should go in your cubby."

A wide smile spread across Molly's face. "My mum made her famous chocolate chip cookies!" replied Molly. "I'm keeping them safe."

"Safe from what?" Kayley asked.

"Snack bandits," Molly whispered. She looked from side to side. "They could be lurking anywhere. They sneak around and steal snacks. That's why Mr Rose keeps his sweets hidden. He hides them in the top drawer of his desk. He thinks we don't know they're there."

Kayley looked under her desk. She looked around the room. "I don't see any snack bandits," she whispered back.

"They are always in disguise," Molly said. "I should ask Mr Rose if I can lock my cookies in the school safe. That's where they keep unchewed rubbers and felt-tips that aren't dried up. You know, valuable things."

"Hey! Where is Mr Rose?" Kayley asked.

Mr Rose was not in the room.

"Mr Rose is **ALWAYS** here in the morning," Molly said. "He stands in the doorway and drinks coffee. He waves and says hello. And he drinks more coffee. He asks how we are. Then he drinks more coffee."

"Yeah," Kayley said. "Where do you think he is?"

"Maybe he had a coffee emergency," Molly said. "Maybe he locks his extra coffee in the school safe with the rubbers and felt-tips. He's probably at the safe getting more coffee."

"There he is!" Kayley cried.

Mr Rose walked through the door. A new girl slipped in behind him. She was holding a Silly Squirrel lunch box. "Class, I'd like you to meet our new pupil, Tori," Mr Rose said. "Please make her feel welcome."

Tori waved nervously at the class.

"Hey!" Kayley cried. "I have the same lunch box as the new kid!"

"Hmmm," Molly said. "A new kid comes on the same day I bring my mum's famous chocolate chip cookies. Doesn't that seem strange? She could be a secret snack bandit!"

"Don't be silly, Molly," said Kayley.

Molly pointed at Tori's top. "Look at her top. It has the letters S.B. on it. They must stand for Snack Bandit!"

"A snack bandit would not have that printed on her top," said Kayley. "That would give her away."

Mr Rose lead Tori to the empty desk in front of Kayley.

"Molly and Kayley, I'd like you to show Tori around today. It's not easy starting at a new school."

"Hi, Tori!" Kayley said. "We have the same lunch box!"

Tori smiled and slipped into the empty seat. "I love Silly Squirrel," she said.

"Me, too!" Kayley said. "I have Silly Squirrel sheets. I have a Silly Squirrel beach towel, too."

"Is it the towel with the picture of Silly Squirrel surfing?" asked Tori.

"Yes!" Kayley squealed.

"I have that same exact towel!" Tori said.

Kayley and Tori both clapped and laughed.

Molly carefully peeked into her lunch box. She wanted to make sure her cookies were safe.

Tori leaned over and pointed. "Ooh, I **LOVE** cookies," she said.

Molly quickly closed her lunch box. She stuffed it into her desk.

Mr Rose walked over to Tori. "Ms Siano needs to see you, Tori," he said. "You left your jumper in the office. It's just down the corridor."

Mr Rose walked Tori to the door. He pointed at the office.

Molly leaned over. She tapped Kayley's shoulder. "I'm pretty sure the new girl is really a snack bandit. Did you see her eyeing my cookies?"

Kayley shook her head. "She was just trying to talk to you," she replied.

Molly sighed. "I think she wants to steal my cookies."

"You think Tori came to a new school just to steal your cookies?" Kayley asked. "How would she even know about your cookies?"

Molly nodded. "These are my mum's **FAMOUS** cookies," she replied. "That means everybody knows about them. Especially snack bandits. They probably have some kind of snack bandit newsletter. I need to keep my eye on her."

"She's nice," said Kayley. "I really don't think she is going to steal your cookies, Molly."

"You're right," Molly said. She checked to make sure her lunch box was still safe in her desk. "Because I won't let her."

Chapter 2

What's Worse Than a Snack Bandit?

Rrrrrrrrriiiinnnnnnngggg!

The bell rang for breaktime. Molly grabbed her lunch box. She stuffed it under her hoodie. Then she put her hood up. She pulled it tight around her face.

"Molly Mac?" asked Mr Rose as she crept past his desk.

Molly froze and stared. "How did you see me?" she asked. "I'm in super secret snack protection mode."

Mr Rose tapped his glasses. "X-ray glasses," he said. "All teachers have them."

Molly nodded. "That would explain a lot," she replied.

"Now, maybe you can tell me why you are creeping around. Why is your lunch box stuffed under your hoodie?" Mr Rose asked.

"Snack bandits," Molly whispered.

"Ahhh, I see." Mr Rose took a sip of his coffee. He crossed a day off of his desk calendar. "Only 124 days left until the summer holidays. Why don't you go out and play, Molly."

Molly slipped out of the door onto the playground. She ran to the secret spot. It was where she ate snacks with Kayley every day. She sat down and pulled her hood off. "I think we lost her!" she cried.

"Lost who?" Tori asked.

Molly looked up and stared at Tori. "You!" she cried. "What are **YOU** doing in our secret snack spot?"

Kayley and Tori both laughed. "We're eating our snacks!" they said together.

Molly pointed at her lunch box. "Stay away from my cookies," she said. "Are you a snack bandit?"

"Snack bandit?" Tori laughed. "I'm not a snack bandit."

"Then why are the letters S.B. on your T-shirt?" Molly asked.

Tori turned around. She showed Molly the back of her T-shirt. It had a big picture of a horse on it. "S.B. stands for Sunnyvale Barn," Tori said. "That's where I used to ride horses."

Molly grabbed her cookies. She held them up. "You said you **LOVE** cookies. Did you come here to steal my cookies?"

Tori shook her head. "They look delicious," she said. "But I wouldn't steal your snack. And look! My mum made cookies, too!" Tori held up a bag of cookies. "I gave one to Kayley. Would you like one?"

Molly shook her head. "No, thank you."

"I told you she wasn't a snack bandit, Molly," said Kayley. "Come on, Tori. I'll show you the best swing to use."

Kayley and Tori ran towards the swings.

Molly watched them laughing and playing together. She took a bite of a cookie. "Tori isn't a snack bandit. She's a best friend bandit," she said to herself.

Chapter 3

Gloppy Joes

After breaktime, Molly slumped in her seat.

"Okay, class, please line up for art," said Mr
Rose.

Kayley and Tori rushed to line up.

"Come on, Molly!" Kayley said. "It's time
for art!"

Molly reached into her desk. She pretended
to look for something. "I'll be right there,
Mr Rose," she said.

Mr Rose lead the class down the corridor. A
few minutes later, he was back in the classroom.
He saw Molly sitting with her head on her desk.

"Don't ask," said Molly.

"I'm asking," said Mr Rose.

Molly sighed. "I thought Tori was a snack bandit," she said. "I thought she came to steal my mother's famous cookies. But I was wrong. She's a best friend bandit. And she's stealing Kayley from me."

"I don't think anyone could ever steal Kayley from you, Molly," he said. "I've been a teacher for a long time. I've seen a lot of friends. You and Kayley are two of the best friends I have ever seen."

"You don't think Kayley will forget about me?" Molly asked.

"I don't think anyone could ever forget you, Molly," he answered.

Molly smiled. "Thanks, Mr Rose," she replied. Molly skipped out of the door to art.

Riiiiiiiiiinnnnnnng!!!

The lunch bell rang.

"Sloppy joes! Sloppy joes! Sloppy joes!" Molly sang. She raced through the crowded hallway to the canteen.

Mr Rose stepped in front of her. He held out
his hand. "How many times have I talked to you
about running in the corridor?" he asked.

"Is this a maths test?" Molly asked.
"Because it's sloppy joe day at lunch. I can't be
late. The sandwiches get all gloppy by the end.
Then it's a gloppy joe. And that's not the same
thing at all. Nobody likes gloppy joes."

"Walk in the corridor, Molly," Mr Rose said.

Molly walked to the canteen. She queued up.

"Hello, Molly," said Dinner Lady Deb.

"Hi, Dinner Lady Deb," replied Molly. "Mr Rose made me walk. Are the joes gloppy or sloppy?"

Schlrrrrrrrrrp!

Dinner Lady Deb stirred the giant, steaming pot. She scooped a heaping pile onto Molly's tray. "Definitely sloppy," she said.

"**Woo! Hoo!**" Molly cheered. She carried her tray across the canteen.

"**Kayley! Kayley! The joes are still sloppy!**" cried Molly. "I made it in time! Even though Mr Rose made me walk. Now we can–"

Molly stopped and stared. Tori was sitting in Molly's spot.

Molly squinted her eyes. "That's my seat," she grumbled.

Tori turned bright red. She grabbed her lunch box. "I didn't know you had assigned seats at lunch," she said. "Sorry, Molly."

Kayley laughed. "We don't have assigned seats," she said. "But Molly always sits there. Molly, just sit over here instead."

Kayley pointed to the seat across from her.

"But I always sit next to you," Molly said.

"Today you can sit across from me!" Kayley said. She pointed to her lunch box. "I forgot that it was sloppy joe day. My mum packed me a lunch."

"But we **ALWAYS** have sloppy joes together!" Molly said. "We're Sloppy Joe Buddies."

"My mum packed me a lunch today, too," Tori said. "Leftover pizza!"

She opened her lunch box. Then she pulled out a slice of cold pizza. She had a bag of carrot sticks and a yoghurt, too.

"I have leftover pizza, too!" Kayley said. She lifted a slice of pizza from her lunch box. "Extra cheese!"

"Mine, too!" cried Tori.

"We can be Extra Cheese Pizza Buddies!"
Kayley said.

Kayley and Tori laughed.

Molly poked at her lunch until it turned
gloppy.

Chapter 4

The Phone Call

Bang!

Molly stomped into the house after school. She slammed the door behind her.

"**Shhhhhhh!**" Mum hissed. She pointed to the couch. "I just got Alex to sleep."

Molly scowled and flopped down in a chair.

Mum closed her laptop. She sat on the arm of the chair next to Molly. "Rough day, honey?" she asked.

Molly sighed. "I brought your cookies to school. I kept them safe from the snack bandit."

"Snack bandit?" Mum said. "And who would that be?"

"She was pretending to be a new kid.

But she wasn't really a snack bandit at all.

She's an even worse kind of bandit. She's a

seat-stealing best friend bandit. And she did it.

She bandited my best friend."

"So there's a new girl at school?" Mum asked.

Molly nodded.

Mum hugged Molly and stroked her hair. "Oh, sweetie," she said. "I'll pack an extra cookie for your new friend tomorrow."

"No," Molly said, jumping up from the chair. "I don't need an extra cookie. I don't need ANY cookies. I don't have any friends to share them with anymore. Tori and Kayley are best friends now."

Molly's eyes filled with tears. She dropped her head on her mother's shoulder and cried.

"Oh, sweetheart," Mum said. She patted Molly's hair. "You and Kayley have been best friends forever. And it's always fun to make a new friend. Have you talked to Kayley about it?"

Molly shook her head and sniffed.

"Why don't you just call her?" Mum asked. "You can tell her how you're feeling. I'm sure that will make it better."

Molly trudged over to the phone. She dialled Kayley's number.

"Hello, Mrs Kayley's mum," she said. "This is Molly. May I please speak to Kayley? Oh... umm... okay. Thanks. Goodbye."

"Isn't Kayley home?" Mum asked.

"She's home," Molly said. "She couldn't come to the phone. Tori is over at her house for dinner. They're playing outside."

Molly burst into tears and ran up to her bedroom.

Chapter 5

The Great Idea

Knock. Knock. Knock.

Dad poked his head into Molly's bedroom. "Is anybody home?" he asked.

Molly stuck her head out from under her blanket. "I'm home," she said.

Dad sat down on the edge of Molly's bed. "Mum told me you didn't have a great day," he said.

"I had the worst day ever," Molly said. "Tori, the best friend bandit, came to school. She bandited my best friend. Now they are having dinner. And I'm stuck here with you."

Dad frowned. "Thanks very much!"

"Well, it's just that you are kind of old and boring," said Molly. "Except for Alex. He's young and boring. And drooly. Kayley is more fun and less drooly. But now she has a new best friend."

"Molly, you need to understand something. People can have lots of friends," said Dad. "Kayley can be friends with you and Tori. It's good to have a lot of friends. You can't get upset with Kayley for playing with somebody else."

"It's not just playing," Molly said. "They're Extra Cheese Pizza Buddies. And Kayley is supposed to be my Sloppy Joe Buddy. Plus, Tori is over at Kayley's house right now eating dinner! **That's MY job!**"

Dad smiled and patted Molly's toes under the blankets. He got up and walked to the door. "Your job is to go to school tomorrow and be the best friend you can be," he said. He closed the door behind him.

Molly smiled. She patted her stuffed animal, Bull. "Be the best friend I can be?" she said. "I can do better than that. I'll be the best friend in the entire universe."

Chapter 6

A Long, Long, Long Song

The next day, Molly slipped into the classroom extra early.

Shhhp. Shhhhp. Shhhhhp.

"Do I even want to know what you're doing in here, Molly?" asked Mr Rose.

"Probably not," Molly Mac answered. She was under Kayley's desk. She had a dustpan and a brush. "I had a little accident with the glitter. And now I'm cleaning it up. But this glitter is sticky stuff!"

Mr Rose slowly slurped his coffee. He stood by the door, waiting for the kids to file into the classroom.

Molly crouched down behind her chair. She waited until Tori and Kayley came in.

"Hi, Molly!" Kayley said. "Why didn't you meet us on the playground this morning?"

Molly hopped up from behind her chair. "How did you see me hiding here?" she asked. "Did you get X-ray glasses, too? I was going to jump up and surprise you. But your X-ray glasses sort of ruined that."

Tori smiled. "I love surprises!" she said.

Kayley laughed. "Why are you surprising me?" she asked.

"Because you're **MY** best friend," Molly said. "And I wrote a song about us last night. I wrote it while I was home alone. While you two were having dinner together. Without me. Because I was home. **Alone.** Because nobody invited me over for dinner."

Molly pulled some folded pieces of paper

from her pocket. She climbed up on her chair.

"Down," called Mr Rose from the doorway.

"He didn't even look this way," Molly

whispered. "His X-ray glasses are amazing!"

Molly cleared her throat and sang.

"Kayley, you're my best friend.

And I'm your best friend, too!

I don't want my sloppy joes with anyone but you!

We've been best friends forever.

And will always be best friends.

Even when a new kid moves here. And she tries

to be your best friend. Or she tries to be your Extra

Cheese Pizza Buddy. And goes over to your house for

dinner. And has the same lunch box as you. That

isn't even fair. I don't really even like Silly Squirrel!

Because he's kind of creepy…"

The bell rang.

"Okay, Molly," said Mr Rose. "I think that's
enough singing for the day."

Molly held up the papers in her hand. "I
still have four more pages, Mr Rose," she said.

"Save it for break, Molly," Mr Rose replied.

Chapter 7

The Best Smelling Crown Ever

At breaktime, Molly ran over to the secret snack spot before Tori and Kayley could get there. She put her rucksack on the ground and opened it.

Kayley and Tori ran over.

"Why didn't you wait for us, Molly?" gasped Kayley.

Molly lifted a wrapped package out of her rucksack. Glitter fell from it like raindrops.

"I have a best friend surprise for you, Kayley," Molly said. "Because we are best friends!" She gently handed the package to Kayley. It was soggy and damp.

Kayley opened the package. She took out a
giant, glittery paper crown. It was covered with
hearts and beads. On it were pictures of Molly
and Kayley. Across the front it said, "Molly's
Real Actual Best Friend!!!!!!!" Across the back
it said, "Sloppy Joe Buddies **FOREVER!!!!!!!!**"

"**WOW!**" Kayley said. "It's beautiful!"

"I used all your favourite colours. I'm your best friend. I know what your favourite colours are. And I drew a picture of a sloppy joe! But it looks a little bit like sick. Sloppy joes are **really** hard to draw! And I wanted to glue some macaroni to it. I know you think macaroni always looks fancy. But my mum used all the macaroni for cheesy macaroni last night. So I washed the cheese off some of it. Then I tried to glue it on. But it was kind of soggy. And cheesy."

Kayley sniffed the crown. "It smells delicious," she said. "Your mum makes the best smelling macaroni and cheese."

"Put it on! Put it on!" cried Molly. "Then you'll remember that you are **MY** best friend!"

"I think the glue is still wet," Kayley said. She gently lifted the crown to put it on, but it folded and twisted. It ripped in half.

Glitter, beads, and macaroni fell to the ground. The crown was ruined.

Kayley bent down. She scooped up the pieces of the crown. When she stood up, she smiled at Molly.

Molly sat down and crossed her arms.

Kayley sat next to her.

"It's okay, Molly. I can still sniff its cheesy goodness." She sniffed the crown. "**Mmm. Cheesy.**"

Molly shook her head. "It's not for sniffing. It's for wearing. I wanted you to wear the crown. I want you to remember that you are **MY** best friend. And you're supposed to invite **ME** over to dinner at your house."

Kayley pointed at Tori. "Our dads work together!" she said.

"That's why we moved here," Tori said.

"And my dad invited Tori's family over for dinner last night," Kayley said. "He said it would be nice to make them feel welcome."

Molly glared at Tori. "Welcome to steal my best friend?" she asked.

Tori sat down next to Molly. She burst into tears.

Molly tapped Tori on the shoulder. "Why are you crying?" she asked. "You have a new best friend."

Tori shook her head and sobbed. "I already
have a best friend at my old school. Her name
is Amy. I didn't want a new best friend. I didn't
even want to move. We had to because of my
dad's work. I miss my best friend. I miss my
old house. I miss my old school and all my old
friends. I tried to make new friends. But I made
you mad. Now I won't have any friends at all."

Kayley put her arm around Tori's shoulder. "I'm still your friend," she told her. "And so is Molly! Aren't you, Molly?"

Molly sighed. She poked some soggy macaroni with her toe. "But you guys were doing things without me. Plus you have matching Silly Squirrel lunch boxes."

"You don't even like Silly Squirrel, Molly," Kayley said. "And we'll always be best friends. And now we can be best friends with Tori, too!"

Molly shuffled closer to Tori. She put her arm around her. "Are you sure you're not here to steal my cookies?" she asked.

"I brought my own cookies again," she said. "I brought enough to share with both of you."

"That's good," said Molly. She pointed to her rucksack. "Because I think all the glue, glitter and macaroni ruined my snack."

Tori held out a cookie and smiled.

"Chocolate Chip Cookie Buddies?" she asked.

Kayley and Molly each took a cookie from Tori. "Chocolate Chip Cookie Buddies!" they replied.

Chapter 8

New Rucksack, New Bandit

The next day, Molly plonked down in her seat. "Good news!" she said. "My mum bought me a new rucksack. All the gluey, glittery, cheesy goodness didn't wash out of my old one."

"Is it a Silly Squirrel rucksack?" asked Tori.

"Nope," Molly answered. "Because I still find him a bit creepy. But that's not the best news. This is!" Molly held up her lunch box. "My mum packed me cookies again. And she packed enough for me to share with you! Now that I don't have to worry about you being a snack bandit, we can–"

"Class!" Mr Rose said. He clapped his hands.

Clap. Clap. Clap-clap-clap!

"I have a quick announcement to make," he said. "I have to go to a meeting this morning. Miss Heather will be in the classroom with you until I get back. She usually helps out in Year 4. Please be on your best behaviour."

Molly's eyes grew wide. She clutched her lunch box and whispered to Tori and Kayley. "That's not a new teacher. That's a snack bandit."

She put her lunch box on her seat. She climbed on top of it to protect it.

"Do I even want to know what you're doing, Molly Mac?" asked Mr Rose.

"Probably not," said Molly.

All About Me!

A picture of me!

Name:
Marty Kelley

People in my family:
My lovely wife, Kerri
My amazing son, Alex
My terrific daughter, Tori

I really like: Pizza! And hiking in the woods. And being with my friends. And reading. And making music. And travelling with my family.

When I grow up I want to be:
A rock star drummer!

My special memory:
Sitting on the sofa with my kids and reading a huge pile of books together.

Find more at my website: www.martykelley.com

MOLLY MAC

≥ Tooth Fairy Trouble ≤
by MARTY KELLEY

MOLLY MAC

≥ Lucky Break ≤
by MARTY KELLEY

MOLLY MAC

≥ Sammy's Great Escape ≤
by MARTY KELLEY

For more exciting books from
brilliant authors, follow the fox!
www.curious-fox.com